3

Dad went to feed the horses.

He gave them some hay.

A Windy Day

by **Sue Graves** and **Beccy Blake**

W
FRANKLIN WATTS
LONDON•SYDNEY

It was a windy day
on the farm.

But the wind blew

the hay away.

Gran went to feed the hens.

She gave them some corn.

But the wind blew

the corn away.

Grandad went
to put the washing
on the washing line.

But the wind blew the washing into a tree!

Mum and Dad made everyone
a cup of tea.

"I don't like windy days,"
said Gran.
"We can't do our jobs
on windy days."

"We can't do our jobs,"

said Josh.

"But we can fly my kite."

13

They went outside.

14

The wind blew and blew.

It blew the kite up and up.

Josh held on to the kite.

The wind blew and blew
and blew!

It blew Josh up and up.

They held on to Josh.

"I like windy days," said Gran.

"And I like kites!"

19

Story trail

Start

Start at the beginning of the story trail. Ask your child to retell the story in their own words, pointing to each picture in turn to recall the sequence of events.

Independent Reading

This series is designed to provide an opportunity for your child to read on their own. These notes are written for you to help your child choose a book and to read it independently.

In school, your child's teacher will often be using reading books which have been banded to support the process of learning to read. Use the book band colour your child is reading in school to help you make a good choice. A *Windy Day* is a good choice for children reading at Blue Band in their classroom to read independently.

The aim of independent reading is to read this book with ease, so that your child enjoys the story and relates it to their own experiences.

About the book
It gets very windy on the farm, making all the jobs too hard. Josh finds something everyone can do on a windy day.

Before reading
Help your child to learn how to make good choices by asking:
"Why did you choose this book? Why do you think you will enjoy it?" Look at the cover together and ask: "What do you think the story will be about?" Support your child to think of what they already know about the story context. Read the title aloud and ask: "Where is the story set? What do you think the boy is going to do? " Remind your child that they can try to sound out the letters to make a word if they get stuck.

Decide together whether your child will read the story independently or read it aloud to you. When books are short, as at Blue Band, your child may wish to do both!

During reading

If reading aloud, support your child if they hesitate or ask for help by telling the word. Remind your child of what they know and what they can do independently.

If reading to themselves, remind your child that they can come and ask for your help if stuck.

After reading

Use the story trail to encourage your child to retell the story in the right sequence, in their own words.

Support comprehension by asking your child to tell you about the story. Help your child think about the messages in the book that go beyond the story and ask: "Why was Gran happy at the end of the story?"

Give your child a chance to respond to the story: "Did you have a favourite part? Do you like to fly kites? Why/Why not?"

Extending learning

In the classroom, your child's teacher may be reinforcing punctuation and how it informs the way we group words in sentences.

On a few of the pages, ask your child to find the speech marks that show us where someone is talking and then read it aloud, making it sound like talking. Find the exclamation marks and ask your child to think about the expression they use for exclamations.

Franklin Watts
First published in Great Britain in 2017
by The Watts Publishing Group

Copyright © The Watts Publishing Group 2017

Series Editors: Jackie Hamley and Melanie Palmer
Series Advisors: Dr Sue Bodman and Glen Franklin
Series Designer: Peter Scoulding

A CIP catalogue record for this book is
available from the British Library.

ISBN 978 1 4451 5475 6 (hbk)
ISBN 978 1 4451 5476 3 (pbk)
ISBN 978 1 4451 6082 5 (library ebook)

Printed in China

Franklin Watts
An imprint of
Hachette Children's Group
Part of The Watts Publishing Group
Carmelite House
50 Victoria Embankment
London EC4Y 0DZ

An Hachette UK Company
www.hachette.co.uk

www.franklinwatts.co.uk